THE ADVENTURES OF BUDDY THE BEAVER

MYSTERY OF THE MISSING FRIENDS

Story and Photography by

CARSON AND JIM CLARK

Printed using Soy-based inks
Sustainable Manufacturing
Renewable Resources

Mountain Trail Press is committed to protecting the environment and to the responsible use of natural resources. As a book publisher, with paper a core part of our business, we are concerned about the future of the world's remaining Endangered Forests and the environmental impacts of paper production. We are committed to our recently implemented policies that support the preservation of High Conservation Value Forests globally and advance best practices within the book and paper industries.

We are improving our environmental impact and have eliminated our use of High Conservation Value Forest fiber by adhering to our strict policy guidelines in paper choice to maximize our use of recycled and/or *FSC certified paper.*

The Forest Stewardship Council (FSC) certification system is the only system that is endorsed by the *Environmental Paper Network, World Wildlife Fund, ForestEthics, Natural Resources Defense Council,* and hundreds of other environmental organizations.

THE ADVENTURES OF BUDDY THE BEAVER
MYSTERY OF THE MISSING FRIENDS

Story and Photography by
CARSON AND JIM CLARK

Book design and layout: Jerry D. Greer & Jim Clark
Digital Pre-press: Jerry D. Greer
Editor: Jamie Rappaport Clark

Published by Mountain Trail Press
1818 Presswood Road
Johnson City, TN 37604

Library of Congress Control Number: ~~2010942551~~
International Standard Book Number: 978-0-9844218-8-6
Printed and bound by Pacom Korea, Inc.
Kyonggido, South Korea

MOUNTAIN TRAIL
P R E S S
www.mountaintrailpress.com

'Celebrating America's Most Scenic Places

Acknowledgments

Dad and I would like to thank the following folks who helped us with our Buddy the Beaver Project: my Uncle Norman Clark, my grandmother Pauline Clark, Polly Vance, and Mr. Ron Circe and Dave Clark at Banshee Reeks Nature Preserve. We would also like to thank Jeanne Morency for letting us go with her to photograph the baby red foxes. We thank Caroline Hickman for finding the gray tree frog for us to photograph.

We would also like to thank Mr. Jerry Greer of Mountain Trail Press for publishing our book and to our sponsors Hunts Photo & Video, Lowepro, Manfrotto Imaging, Nik Software, and Wimberley.

Most of all we want to thank Jamie Rappaport Clark, my mom (and Dad's wife!) for all her love, support, and "determined" encouragement to help us get through another book project! Thanks Mom!

About the Authors/Photographers:

Carson has been photographing and speaking about nature since age six. His images have won a host of national and international awards. In 2010 – at the age of ten – Carson was the opening keynote speaker at the annual meeting of the North American Nature Photography Association in Reno, Nevada. Carson has traveled the country with his Dad to speak about nature and photography. Carson is a competitive horseback rider, black belt in Taekwondo, Boy Scout, violinist, and an avid basketball and lacrosse player. This is Carson's second book in his Buddy the Beaver series, a joint nature photography project with his dad.

Jim is a contributing editor for Outdoor Photographer magazine. His articles and photographs have appeared in numerous magazines and he's the author/photographer of five books. Jim was also a major contributor the books, Ultimate Guide to Digital Nature Photography and Coal Country.

To learn more about Carson and Jim, visit www.carsonclarkphoto.com and www.jimclarkphoto.com.

FOR MY MOM

Springtime had arrived at Buddy's pond. Winter's snow was now a memory. Soon, the trees and flowers around the pond would paint the land in a burst of bright, fresh colors.

As Buddy prepared to leave his lodge, he became excited about exploring the pond.

Buddy's lodge was nestled along the bank of the pond. The pond was so large it would take Buddy all day to go from end to the other.

That was okay with Buddy. He loved to explore and if he could, Buddy would do it every day! As Buddy left the lodge and swam to the surface, he saw his mom. "Good morning mom," said Buddy.

" Well, good morning to you Buddy," replied his mother. "Are you ready to explore the pond today?"

"I can't wait to start," answered Buddy as he paddled up to his mom.

Buddy also saw his dad cruising near the lodge. "I just want to see my friends again and play and flip and dive!" Buddy's dad just smiled.

And with a big splash, Buddy dove in to the water and began his journey around the pond.

Throughout the day as Buddy explored the pond, he noticed more and more how quiet it was. Buddy tried hard to listen, but as much as he listened and as much as he looked, he could not hear nor see any of his songbird or frog friends.

"Where are my friends? Why is it so quiet?" Buddy whispered to himself as he swam back to the lodge.

"Mom! Dad!" cried out Buddy as he saw them floating near the lodge.

"I can't hear or see my songbird friends! Why is it so quiet? My friends have disappeared!"

"Come on over here and help me with this branch and I'll tell you all about what is happening," replied Buddy's dad.

Buddy listened as his dad explained that during the winter some birds fly south where the weather is much warmer.

"So, that means that they will come back?" asked Buddy.

"Oh yes, they will," replied his dad. "They return in spring, but not all your songbird friends really left."

"Why not?" asked Buddy.

"Well, some of your friends such as Cards the Cardinal can withstand the cold temperatures of winter," replied Buddy's dad. "But other birds like Renee the Robin fly south. When birds fly south, it is called migration."

For the rest of the day Buddy continued searching the pond for his friends. As Buddy swam, he could see the land around the pond was changing.

The trees in the forest were becoming greener.

Colorful wildflowers such as bluebells were growing along the banks of the pond.

But Buddy still wanted to see his friends. "Where are they?" wondered Buddy. "Do my frog friends migrate, too?" He had forgotten to ask his dad.

As darkness fell, Buddy swam back to the lodge. He was determined to solve the mystery of his missing friends.

The light of the day had almost disappeared from the sky when Buddy suddenly heard a peeping noise from the edge of the pond. "Peep, Peep, Peep," repeated the peeping noise from the edge of the pond.

"Who's that?" asked Buddy. "It's me," replied the peeping noise from the edge of the pond. "Peep, Peep, Peep."

"Where are you?" asked Buddy.

"Down here," came the peeping noise from the edge of the pond.

It was Peeps the Spring Peeper! Peeps is a very small frog.

Buddy and Peeps are very good friends. "Peeps!" said Buddy. "Where have you been? Have you been migrating?"

"Oh no Buddy, I've been hibernating." answered Peeps. "Peep, Peep, Peep."

"What's hibernating?" asked Buddy.

"Hibernation is when frogs like me bury into the mud to avoid the cold winter," answered Peeps. "I go into a deep sleep and wait for the warm weather of spring to arrive. Peep, Peep, Peep."

Just before Buddy dove into the water to enter the lodge, he heard his friend Gary the Gray Tree Frog.

"Trill, Trill, Trill," sang Gary.

"Hey Buddy! Good to see you again!" called out Gary.

"Good to see you too, Gary," replied Buddy. "Have you been hibernating like Peeps?"

"That's right, I have," replied Gary. Like all tree frogs, Gary has big suction pads on his toes to help him cling to trees and branches.

The next morning, Buddy decided to journey to the far side of the pond.

As Buddy neared the end of the pond, he looked up and saw a small, furry creature clinging to the trunk of a tree.

"Who are you?" asked Buddy.

The small furry creature clinging to the tree answered, "I'm Blake the Black Bear Cub."

"Nice to meet you Blake," replied Buddy.

"Where have you been for the winter? Did you hibernate in the mud or migrate south for the winter?"

"Oh no," answered Blake. "I was born in a den this winter. I stayed warm next to my mother while she took care of me."

"I bet you can see a long way from up there," responded Buddy.

"Yes, I can," answered Blake, "I even see Norman the Bald Eagle flying this way."

Buddy looked up at the beautiful blue spring sky and saw his friend Norman gliding overhead.

"Hey Norman!" yelled Buddy. "Did you hibernate this winter like Peeps, and Gary?"

Norman the Bald Eagle turned and circled above him.

"Oh no," answered Norman as he flew overhead. "I stayed here. If it gets cold though, I sometimes fly south to where it is warmer."

Buddy said goodbye to Blake and Norman. Buddy continued his journey and as he turned a corner, he saw two of his friends perched on a bush along the edge of the pond.

It was Brynn and Brenda, the Brown Thrashers. "Hey Brynn and Brenda!" shouted Buddy. "Have you been migrating?"

"Yes we have," sang Brynn.

"We just got back and it is so nice to be at the pond again." Brynn and Brenda were busy gathering twigs and grass to build their nest.

Buddy was so happy to see Brynn and Brenda. As they collected sticks for their nest, Buddy continued his day of exploring.

Suddenly, Buddy heard a "Klee, Klee, Klee" call above him. Buddy looked up and saw Kelli the Kestrel landing at her nest box high on a post in the meadow next to the pond.

"Hey Kelli!" yelled Buddy. "Have you been migrating, too?"

"Hello Buddy," screeched Kelli. "Yes I have."

Like all kestrels, Kelli builds her nest in cavities in old trees or next boxes that humans place on tall posts in the meadow.

"Well, welcome back Kelli," replied Buddy.

Throughout the rest of the day, Buddy began seeing even more of his friends, like Patty the Eastern Phoebe, who also migrated south for the winter. Patty was one of the first songbirds to return for spring.

Also returning was Renee the Robin, who was already on her nest and incubating her newly laid eggs.

Along the edge of the forest Buddy heard the "Rat-A-Tat-Tat" pecking of his friend Ron, the Red-bellied Woodpecker.

"Hey Ron!" cried out Buddy. "Did you hibernate or migrate for the winter?"

"Nope, I stayed here all winter," answered Ron as he kept pecking on the tree stump.

Buddy was so happy to see so many of his friends returning to the pond.

Swimming around another bend in the pond, Buddy saw his friend, Sunflower, the Gray Squirrel. "Sunflower!" yelled Buddy. "It's so good to see you again! Did you migrate or hibernate for the winter?"

Sunflower hopped to the ground. "Good to see you Buddy," chattered Sunflower. "No, I was warm and snug in my tree cavity. On warm winter days I scurried outside to search for acorns. But I'm so glad that winter is over!"

Buddy had finally solved the mystery of his missing friends. His frog friends had stayed in or close to the pond hibernating for the winter.

Some of his bird friends had stayed for the winter, but others migrated south. His mammal friends – those with hair – had hibernated or were able to survive outside in the cold winter.

He was so happy to have everyone back at the pond.

As Buddy turned around to swim back home, he heard voices along the edge of the pond.

Five times he heard, "Hey Buddy!" "Hey Buddy!" "Hey Buddy" Hey Buddy!" "Hey Buddy!"

"Who's that?" asked Buddy.

It's us!" squeaked the voices along the edge of the pond.

Buddy watched as five baby red foxes popped into view.

"I'm Eenie," yelped the first baby red fox.

"I'm Meenie," barked the second baby red fox.

"I'm Mynie," yapped the third baby red fox.

"I'm Moe," shouted the fourth baby red fox.

"And I'm Uh-Oh!" yelled the fifth baby red fox as he stretched his legs.

"We met some of your friends today and they told us all about you. We are so happy to meet you Buddy," said Eenie as Mynie licked her nose.

"Wow!" shouted Buddy, "Nice to meet you Eenie, Meenie, Mynie, Moe, and Uh-Oh. Have you been migrating or hibernating for the winter?"

"Oh no," answered Eenie, Meenie, Mynie, Moe, and Uh-Oh at the same time. "We were born in an underground den earlier this spring."

"This is our first time outside our den," yapped Uh-Oh as he started to yawn.

And with that, Uh-Oh jumped high above the ground. "It's fun to explore springtime!" barked Uh-Oh as he landed.

Eenie, Meenie, Mynie, Moe, and Uh-Oh said goodnight to Buddy as they went into their den for the night.

Buddy continued swimming towards home.

As the sun sank below the western horizon, a full moon came into view in the eastern sky.

Buddy saw his Canada geese friends flying high overhead.

They, too, had migrated south for the winter, but were now returning.

Buddy smiled again. It was so good to see them come home.

The mystifying mystery of his missing friends was finally over.

"It's going to be a great spring!" Buddy whispered to himself as he entered the lodge.

Indeed it will, Buddy. Indeed it will.

The End

Here are Buddy's friends that he saw on his journey around the pond. Can you point out which ones migrate, hibernate, or stay for the winter?

[8]